ALULA-BELLE
BRAVES ICE CREAM BEACH

ALULA-BELLE
BRAVES ICE CREAM BEACH

Cover illustration by Marie Chapian
Book Design: Jon Ritt

Published by Bethany House Publishers
A Ministry of Bethany Fellowship, Inc.
11300 Hampshire Avenue South
Minneapolis, Minnesota 55438
95 - 43840
Printed in the United States of America

FOR CHRISTA

CONTENTS

...talking to a blue jay and having a favorite think.

CHAPTER I

ALULA-BELLE LEARNS OF A PROBLEM

It happened this way: One fine Tuesday or Saturday, or maybe Wednesday, Alula-Belle Button-Top Paintbrush Softshoe Pucheeni Magrew sat in a tree talking to a blue jay and having herself a favorite think.

She was thinking about her butterfly family. (I'm sure you remember that Alula-Belle's mother is a beautiful black-and-gold Monarch butterfly. And if you don't, it's positively true.)

Alula-Belle's mother gave her the name Alula, which means Winged One. Of course, Alula-Belle doesn't have wings, but nobody worries about that. Especially since she flies quite well without them.

Alula-Belle liked to think about butterflies because they always smile. Nothing seems to bother butterflies. If a flower has a frown on its face or if it sticks out its tongue, a butterfly goes right on smiling until the flower finally smiles, too.

If a cranky blue jay tries to have a butterfly for its dinner, the butterfly simply laughs and flies away. That's just what Alula-Belle was thinking when who should fly by but her cousin Fred.

"Hi-dee-hi-hi, Fred!" Alula-Belle gave her cousin a kiss on the tip of his antenna. "Delighted you came to visit."

"Hi-dee-hi-hi to you, too, Cousin Alula-Belle," said Fred, shivering his wings. The blue jay gave a loud caw and flew away. Fred watched until it was out of sight.

"Wait'll you hear my news," Fred blurted in an excited voice. "It's terrible! It's an Emergency."

"It's about Ice Cream Beach!" exclaimed Fred in his high butterfly voice.

He sighed and rested on a branch as though he was going to take a nap.

"How about a swig of peach nectar first?" Alula-Belle offered. "Then you can tell me all about the Emergency."

"Peachy," said Fred, with a nod. "Perfectly peachy."

Alula-Belle smiled. "Let's go inside my House Beautimous, which I built myself." She poured a big swig of peach nectar from the old leather boot in the corner. (She had found the boot one day in a clump of moss by the river. It was a very old and dirty boot, but Alula-Belle had cleaned it up. Perfect for pouring perfectly peachy peach nectar!)

"Delicious! Ever so delicious!" Fred said, taking a swig of the cool nectar.

"Now tell me your news, Cousin Fred," said Alula-Belle.

"So terrible. Just terrible!" said Fred. "Big problem. *Terrible* problem. You must do something. And fast, before it's too late."

Alula-Belle, who is famous for problem solving, waited for Fred to explain.

"It's about Ice Cream Beach!" exclaimed Fred in his high butterfly voice.

Ice Cream Beach is a wonderful place in the Chocolate Cliffs along the Ice Cream Sea. The lovely waves rolling upon the sand are not water, but strawberry, chocolate, and pistachio ice cream, with an occasional lap of tutti-frutti—usually in July. Ice cream fills the sea as far as the eye can see. Miles and miles of ice cream. When Alula-Belle was a little girl, it was her favorite place to surf.

But what could the trouble be?

"Somebody—or something—is dumping *pickle juice* into the ice cream!" Fred said with a crackle in his voice.

"Pickle juice!" exclaimed Alula-Belle.

"Pickle juice," repeated Fred. He looked around Alula-Belle's tree house for some pollen to sit on. Alula-Belle offered him her best pollen pillow.

"Cousin, you've got to do something. The sea will be contaminated!"

Jo-Jo Peach Jam, Alula-Belle's Very Smart Turtle, piped up. "But 'contaminate' means *poison*. Who would want to poison Ice Cream Beach?"

Cousin Fred waved four or seven of his arms in the air. "All I know," he said to Jo-Jo, "is that there is a band of Pickle Necks in the area. It looks as if they are the ones dumping buckets and buckets of pickle juice into the ice cream!"

"The Pickle Necks!" exclaimed Alula-Belle and Jo-Jo Peach Jam at once.

The Pickle Necks are feared near and far for their mean deeds. They are big bullies. They push people off swings, they smudge the words on library books, and they eat all the cake at parties—and worse. There is practically no limit to their bad ways.

Alula-Belle offered her cousin another swig of cool peach nectar from the big leather boot in the corner. Soon the sun would be high in the sky. A huge flood of heat would drop down over the forest.

Cousin Fred sipped his nectar. "The Pickle Necks are a menace, I'm afraid," he sighed. "They're sneaky and dangerous. They have somehow discovered Ice Cream Beach. It could mean doom for one of the Seven Most Delicious Wonders of the World. Oh, Cousin, will you help?" There was a glimmer in his eye.

Of course Alula-Belle would help. "In the mood for a triple-treat ice-cream yummer, Jo-Jo?"

Jo-Jo Peach Jam became very excited. He

remembered exactly where the surf divided into twenty-three or forty-eight flavors. He began to figure out how deep the peanut butter marshmallow ice cream went before hitting the cookie crumb fudge, his favorite yummer.

"There are certain precautions we must take when we're up against those Pickle Necks," Alula-Belle stressed. "They are a bad bunch. They never tell the truth."

"And one more thing," said Cousin Fred in a serious voice, "be *sure* you head back long before the sun sets. You have only until sunset tonight. There is a big storm traveling in from the north. You won't be able to fly back after the darkness falls."

"We will take all precautions," said Jo-Jo, who always took such warnings as matters of great importance. Cousin Fred took a last swig of peach nectar, said his goodbyes, and flew out the window. His beautiful wings shimmered bright gold in the morning light.

C H A P T E R

PREPARING FOR TAKE-OFF

Alula-Belle packed everything she needed in her pockets. Jo-Jo traveled with his house on his back, so they were ready to go in a flash.

But as they were preparing to take off, there was a shout from below. It was Pearl Pox, the girl next door, who was too lazy to climb up the tree ladder. She was always spying around, trying

She was too lazy to climb up the tree ladder.

to get information about people. Especially about Alula-Belle. She thought Alula-Belle was the most peculiar person she had ever met.

Pearl Pox watched Jo-Jo Peach Jam folding his beach towel. "Aha! You're going to the beach! I want to come with you. Take me! Take me!"

(Perhaps you remember me telling you about Pearl Pox? She's the ten-year-old daughter of the Pox family next door. She's the girl who doesn't like anything—disagreeable from the outside in. She feeds cat food to the dog and bones to the bird. She doesn't know one song by heart and always interrupts adults when they are talking.)

"Sure, come along, Pearl," invited Alula-Belle cheerfully. "Hi-dee-ho!"

Pearl Pox ran back home to collect her things for the beach. She packed her beach ball, boogie board, tanning lotion, umbrella, sun hat, water wings, pail, and shovel. She packed her snorkel, lemon juice, sunglasses, radio, and lunch. She brought one thornberry-salad sandwich on pumperstump bread, a cup of bramble relish, and a pint of pepper pudding. But Pearl Pox didn't bring anything to share with her friends. No ball or Frisbee, and no lunch, either. Not even a toothpick.

When Alula-Belle saw Pearl's pile of things to take on their journey, she said there was only one problem.

"What's that?" asked Pearl Pox in her surly way.

"You'll have to carry your things all by yourself."

Pearl Pox was angry. "How very selfish of you, Alula-Belle! Thinking of yourself when there is someone who needs a helping hand! Humph!" She humphed and phumphed and humphed some more. "Well, at least get me back in time for dinner. My mother is cooking Spiky Spinach Liver Soup. It's my favorite, and you can't have any. So there!" She stuck her nose in the air. "By the way, how far away is this place we're going to?"

"It's in another country. Far, far away—across the room, at least."

Pearl Pox thought for a moment. "Across the room? What kind of place is that? You are always making things up, Alula-Belle. I don't like it one bit! There is no country on the other side of the room. You mean the other side of the *ocean*, of course. That's what you mean."

"Have it your way," said Alula-Belle. She felt like flying. Butterflies are never bothered by

"There is only one problem."

troublesome details. You'll never catch two butterflies fussing and complaining about matters. Especially not about how far it is across the room.

Alula-Belle sang a little song.

Sky-fly high,
flutter-bye bong.
Better climb aboard
if you want to come along!

3

LOST AMONG
THE UMBRELLA TREES

As they flew out the window, Pearl Pox suddenly screamed a horrible scream. She had completely forgotten she was afraid of high places. She was the kind of person who never climbed trees or played on the swings. She didn't hang from her knees on the bars at school, and she never even went near the shiny red-and-yellow

She had completely forgotten she was afraid of high places.

Ferris wheel at the Kneebend County Fair.

Alula-Belle laughed. Why would anyone be afraid of high places, she wondered. Such a pleasant place to be.

"Where are you taking me?" Pearl Pox screamed, clinging to Alula-Belle's magic boots for dear life. (I'll tell you about Alula-Belle's magic boots in another story.) "Put me down this instant!"

Pearl's allergies were beginning to act up. She was getting ready to sneeze. Pearl Pox always sneezed when she was upset. She did a lot of sneezing and wheezing and blowing her nose.

Jo-Jo Peach Jam was busy writing notes in his notebook. "Those are *cumulus* clouds," he announced. "You can tell because they are fluffy like cauliflower. There are ten types of clouds, and they give us messages about weather. It seems the wind is northwesterly today—"

"Oh no," muttered Pearl Pox. "I'm trapped high in the sky with a crazy girl and a weather turtle!"

Alula-Belle flew
and flew
and flew.
Pearl Pox complained
and complained
and complained.

Jo-Jo tried to cheer Pearl Pox up. "Alula-Belle can fly as far as the rain," he offered shyly.

"No, she can't."

"Yes, she can."

"Can not."

"Can too."

"Can *not*," said Pearl.

"Can *too*," said Jo-Jo.

Alula-Belle was not listening to the argument. She was too busy thinking of a way to stop the Pickle Necks from dumping their pickle juice into the Ice Cream Sea. There just *had* to be a way. She would need Jo-Jo and Pearl's help. And there wasn't much time.

"I'm hungry," said Pearl with a pout. "It's past my lunchtime! I want to eat my lunch!"

"So eat," Alula-Belle answered. "That's what you should do when you're hungry—if at all possible."

"But I can't eat up here in the air. It's too

You can become hopelessly lost in Umbrella Forest.

bumpy. I'll spill. My mother doesn't like it when I spill."

"Have it your way," said Alula-Belle, and she pointed her little button nose down for a landing.

"Hey, wait a minute!" alerted Jo-Jo. "That's the Umbrella Forest down there. It's dangerous. People get hopelessly lost in those umbrella trees."

Alula-Belle gave a laugh and down they went for a slippery-smooth landing on the silky tops of the tall umbrella trees. Down, down they went from high in the sky *here* to to low in the Umbrella Trees *here*.

"Now you've done it, Alula-Belle!" Pearl bellowed. "My lemon juice has leaked all over my brand new bathing suit. And my thornberry-salad sandwich is all soggy."

"Don't worry, Pearl," said Alula-Belle. "I'll pick you a juicy peach."

Pearl Pox was really impatient now. "There are no peach trees here, you peculiar girl. There are only umbrella trees!"

"Have it your way."

Alula-Belle looked around. "I believe this must be the It-Could-Rain Forest. What do you think, Jo-Jo?"

Jo-Jo agreed. "I think it would be wise not to

remain here too long." Then he slipped inside his house to spread some peach jam on his bread and take his vitamins.

"Don't forget, we still have a big problem to solve!" he called out.

"Of course," said Alula-Belle thoughtfully. "The Pickle Necks!"

"What are you talking about, you foolish girl?" asked Pearl Pox. "Are you going to tell me there are pickle trees here in this place?"

"Pickle trees—that's it!" shouted Alula-Belle.

"Pickle trees!" She did a little soft-shoe dance around a Galoshes Bush.

"Come along, passengers, time for take-off!"

But when they were ready for take-off, Alula-Belle remembered something.

"What do you remember?" asked Jo-Jo.

"I remember that I forgot."

"Forgot *what*?" asked Pearl Pox.

"Forgot which way to fly."

"Oh no!" screamed Pearl. Her face was red and blotchy, like she was breaking out in a case of mouths all over her face. "We're lost, are we?" The blotches were now as big as elbows. "Well,

you'll never get me up in the air again—I'll tell you that right now. I'm staying right here." Then she began to sneeze. "I want to go to the beach!" She waved her arms and kicked a rock with a big *ah-choo*.

"How nice," said Alula-Belle. "A little dance always helps a person to think."

Jo-Jo Peach Jam began playing his harmonica.

Pearl Pox blew her nose and sat down to eat her pepper pudding.

Suddenly, there was a loud crash in the bushes. Everyone jumped in surprise.

4

VERA BEARA

T hey heard a voice. It was more like a
loud yawn. *Yaaawn* went the voice.

Pearl Pox hid behind the galoshes bush.
"Yawn, yawn, sleepy me
snoring soundly in a tree—
oh phooey kablooey!"
The voice changed into a roar.

"WHAT'S ALL THAT RACKET? WHO WOKE ME UP? WHO IS DOING ALL THAT SNEEZING? WHO? WHAT? WHERE? WHO? WHO?"

Alula-Belle made a running leap toward the bushes to find the creature belonging to the voice.

Pearl Pox let out a shriek. "Stay away from those bushes!" she cried. She couldn't stop sneezing and wheezing and blowing her nose. "It could be dangerous! *I* could get hurt!"

Alula-Belle laughed. "Don't worry," she called. "I have everything above control." She rushed into the thicket with Jo-Jo Peach Jam riding on her head. "Hi-dee-hi-hi!" she whispered into the darkness. "It's me, Alula-Belle Button-Top Paintbrush Softshoe Pucheeni Magrew!"

All at once there was a loud roar and a loud stomping. Then there was a big ARG and an ARGLY and an ARGLY BARGLY and an ARGLY BARGLY SNARGLY WARGLY. A huge, furry head poked out of the brush.

"Hi-dee-hi-hi," said Alula-Belle with a smile.

"Argle bargle," said the Something.

Alula-Belle hopped on one foot in amazement. "You're a bear!" she said.

"Yes, I am a bear," said the Something bear.

"I am a bear everywhere. In my nose and my toes and my hair, I'm a bear."

"I am a bear everywhere. In my nose and my toes and my hair, I'm a bear."

"Then we can't call you a Something, can we? We must call you Bear!" Alula-Belle was delighted. Jo-Jo Peach Jam made a note in his notebook. Pearl Pox stepped back, just to be safe.

"It's hot and I'm vera vera sleepy," said the bear. "An awful noise like sneezing woke me up." The bear yawned a sleepyish, hotish yawn.

"We shall call you Vera Beara!" pronounced Alula-Belle.

Pearl Pox stuck out her tongue. "That's dumb," she said. "Besides, bears don't sleep in the summer. They sleep in the winter. Vera Beara, you are the most idiotic bear I ever heard of. Besides, there's nothing wrong with my sneezing. I have allergies. Doesn't everyone have allergies?"

Vera Beara scratched her head. "I'm all confused. Do you know what day it is?"

Pearl wiggled her finger in Vera Beara's face. "I'll have you know we've come from all the way across the room!" She took a big bite out of her thornberry-salad sandwich on pumperstump bread. "What have *you* got to be confused about?"

Vera Beara cried big, wet tears. "There was a hole in my umbrella tree, and my cave flooded

in the rain. Oh, I am sad! Is it winter yet?"

"Cheer up." Alula-Belle smiled. "We're here to help you. We're your friends."

"Don't look at *me*," snapped Pearl Pox. "*I* won't be your friend. Don't even think about it. I hate meeting new people. And I especially do not like bears who don't know when it's time to be awake and when it's time to sleep. Go away. Shoo!"

Alula-Belle ignored Pearl Pox and gave Vera Beara a big hug. You might say she gave her a bear hug. "Come along with us. We're going to Ice Cream Beach. We have some business to tend to. I'm sure it will be a lovely day."

Pearl Pox stomped her foot on the ground. "The day is half gone," she groaned. "Does this mean the lovely half is over, or the ugly half is over? Which half is about to begin? The ugly half or the lovely half? Can you tell me that? I want to go home!"

"Oh dear," said Jo-Jo Peach Jam, "my notes tell me that the logistics don't coincide with the mapotomy of the landscape. That is to say, we can't go home."

"And why not, Mr. Smarty-Hat Turtle?"

"Because in the balance between here and there, up and down, in and out, over and about— we are *lost*."

Alula-Belle laughed and did a soft-shoe dance. Shuffling and hopping across the rubbery grass, she patted her buttons, pointed to the sky, and sang,

How can you ever be lost
when it's ever so plain to see
that you are exactly right where you are
and where you left yourself off to be?
Pearl Pox sneezed and stuck her tongue out,

but Alula-Belle continued her song.
When I think I am lost,
I look down and see,
why, I am very much here
and ever so much still me!

C H A P T E R

ICE CREAM BEACH

Off they went—Alula-Belle, Jo-Jo Peach Jam, Pearl Pox, and Vera Beara. Through the sky, over the trees, beyond the shadowy mountains, and across the deep, lonely valleys until—

"There it is!" shouted Alula-Belle.

"I don't see anything," said Pearl Pox. "Just a stupid old beach and a big fat old ocean. I see water every day in my tubbie at home, where I have my rubber boat and my rubber chicken and—oh, my goodness! Can it be? Oh, my goodness!"

Pearl Pox was flabbergasted. Stunned. "That's no ordinary ocean! It's filled entirely with...*ice cream*!" Her mouth began to water.

"I believe I see vanilla pineapple swirl—and look, there's a huge wave of caramel nut!"

"Last stop, Ice Cream Beach!" Alula-Belle announced as she came in for a landing on the sugary soft sand. "My mother used to take me here before she went back to work flying full time."

Pearl Pox could hardly believe her eyes. "Ice...ice cream...ice cream!" Ice cream was the

one thing in this world Pearl Pox actually liked. She loved ice cream. She adored ice cream. She was crazy for ice cream. And here was an entire ocean of it!

Pearl ran to the surf's edge. Squealing with joy, eating, slurping, and burping, she paddled out to the vanilla pineapple swirl. Then she dove into the caramel nut and the strawberry revel and the maple nut tutti-frutti and the praline pecan fudgie wudgie. She gobbled as fast as she could. She gobbled and gobbled and slurped and burped, and paddled and paddled and gobbled and paddled and slurped some more.

Vera Beara slid into the butterscotch chip to cool off. (Bears get hot, too, you know.) "With all

this fur, it's very difficult to get a tan," she sighed, floating on her back. She nibbled at the banana raspberry. "Delicious!"

"It's a tasty snackment, don't you agree?" chuckled Alula-Belle. "Absolutely yummerly!"

Alula-Belle and Jo-Jo splashed first in the blueberry, then in the pistachio. When Jo-Jo discovered the peaches-'n-cream waves, he dove in and stayed there, swimming on his stomach the way turtles like to do.

Alula-Belle was glad everyone was having a good time. It was always nice to see people happy and enjoying themselves. But, wait a minute—what was that terrible taste? Ugh! *Phew!*

The praline pecan tasted like—what? PICKLE JUICE!

The fun was over. The Pickle Necks were definitely nearby.

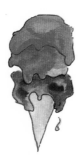

It was always nice to see people happy and having a good time.

THE ATTACK OF THE PICKLE NECKS

Alula-Belle held her breath and swam under ice cream to survey the situation. When she surfaced at the side of the beach, which was usually butterscotch but was now pickle, she saw them. A whole army of Pickle Necks on the beach—looking mean as could be. Then she saw Pearl. She had her nose in the air and was walking toward the Pickle Necks.

A sinister Pickle Neck was just about to attach a KICK ME sign on Pearl's backside. But Pearl caught him in the act.

"Oh, you just try it, you salty vinegar excuse for a pickle!" And she kicked him so hard, he went flying into a wafer dune neck-first. "I'll show you who kicks who, Cucumber Head!"

Another Pickle Neck bully saw Jo-Jo Peach Jam as he emerged from the ice cream and began

his slow turtle walk across the warm, sweet sand.

"Hey, what's this?" squealed the Pickle Neck. "A turtle wearing a top hat!" The other Pickle Necks laughed crazily. "But his hat is just what I need to protect my beautiful green skin from the sun!" With a hoot and a grunt, the Pickle Neck snatched Jo-Jo's hat from his little turtle head and put it on his own lumpy green head.

All at once there was the most ferocious whirlwind you ever saw. It was so loud and so fierce it nearly made pickle relish out of the old Pickle Neck. It was Alula-Belle! She had no trouble at all returning Jo-Jo's hat to him.

"So that's the way it's going to be, is it?" yammered the leader of the Pickle Necks. "Get ready to fight!"

"Have it your way," said Alula-Belle.

The Pickle Necks drew into a huddle. "We'll

get rid of these intruders quick and easy," said the leader (whose name was Marvin, and who happened to be a very tough pickle—an expert in Frisbee, Foos ball and karate).

"Attack!" shouted Marvin Pickle Neck, and the army of Pickle Necks charged toward Alula-Belle and her friends. Vera Beara, who had been washing her feet in the blueberry waves and trying to get a tan on her furry cheeks, saw them

coming. She rose quickly to meet them.

"Say!" she called out to the attacking Pickle Necks, "do any of you boys happen to know what month this is? Might it be December yet?"

The Pickle Necks stopped dead in their tracks. "A *bear*!" They screamed and ran for cover. But since there was no cover to run for, they ran into one another.

If there is one thing Pickle Necks are afraid of in this wide world, it's bears. You just say the word "bear" to a Pickle Neck, and they go flip-flop nuts. That's the truth.

"Bears! *Eeek*!"

Vera Beara tried to remember her manners. "How do you do," she began. "Actually, my name is..."

"Vera Beara," Jo-Jo reminded her gently.

"Yes, Vera Beara," said Vera Beara.

The sky was gathering around the sun in bright orange and purple colors. Soon the sun would set and it would be evening. Jo-Jo Peach Jam looked concerned. "Alula-Belle! Remember your cousin Fred's warning about the storm. Time is running out."

Vera Beara's furry face grew pale. "Did you say time is running out? Oh dear! Where is it going? I have been looking for it so very long. Have you seen it? Is it around here? Hallooo! Time! Where are you?"

"Say, do any of you boys happen to know what month this is?"

Pearl Pox threw ice-cream balls at the Pickle Necks. "Back! Back! Heel!" she yelled.

The Pickle Necks tried to figure out a new plan. "Keep that bear *away* from us!" screamed Marvin Pickle Neck.

Vera Beara lumbered eagerly toward the Pickle Necks. She didn't know that they could be dangerous. She opened her huge paws to them and asked, "But isn't there one of you who knows the month, the week, or when winter will be upon us?"

"Stay away! *Help*!"

Alula-Belle stepped forward with her hands on her hips. She raised one eyebrow and tapped her toe.

"Well well well well well well well," she said in a very adult voice. "I think I'll tell this wild beast of a bear to eat you all up! What do you think of that? Hmmmm?"

"Yes! What do you think of that?" shouted Pearl Pox and Jo-Jo together.

"No! Please, have m-mercy," cried the Pickle Necks.

"Tell me, why I should have mercy on you?" asked Alula-Belle in a most serious voice. "Look what you've done to Ice Cream Beach! You've dumped pickle juice into the ice cream! Yuk!"

"Yes, yuk," added Pearl, "Yucky icky!"

The Pickle Necks couldn't help but giggle their nasty giggle. They were proud of their bad deeds. "Aren't we nasty? Nasty is the only word for us!" And they cackled nastily.

"Dumb heads—that's what you are!" shouted Pearl Pox. "Sour puss pickle twerps!" and she threw a glob of butter pecan at them. It hit Bert, by far the meanest of all Pickle Necks, smack in the neck.

"Ouch! I'll get you for that!" he bellowed.

"I dare you!" yelled Pearl. "I double dare you! I triple dare you! I quadruple dare you! I billionuple-zillion dare you!"

The ice cream went zinging through the air a mile a minute.

"But what about my question?" cried Vera Beara. "Won't somebody answer my question?"

At the sound of Vera Beara's booming voice, the Pickle Neck army cowered back. They shrank, sort of like a paper bag when there's nothing in it.

SPLATT

"Question?"

Alula-Belle jumped forward. "Yes! And the question is, what will you give if I stop this bear from eating you all up?"

"Uh...er...uh." The army was terribly nervous. It's hard to speak when you're that nervous.

Vera Beara yawned a loud yawn. It was loud enough to shake the entire beach and then some. YAAAWN.

"Where are your manners, Ms. Bear?" snapped Pearl Pox to the bear. "Cover your mouth."

The Pickle Necks were so frightened by Vera Beara's yawn that they fell backward all together in a faint.

The ice cream went zinging through the air a mile a minute.

"I'm giving you one more chance," called Alula-Belle in the stern voice school teachers use when you don't do your homework. "Are you ready to talk?" She sounded *real* serious.

"Yes, we're ready for anything," whimpered Marvin Pickle Neck. "We'll do anything you want. And I'm not lying."

But Pickle Necks are big liars.

CHAPTER 7

ALULA-BELLE'S TRICK

Almost everyone knows that Pickle Necks lie from morning till night. If you trust one single word a Pickle Neck says, you're in for it.

"Are you *sure* you'll do anything at all?" Alula-Belle asked Marvin, the Pickle Neck leader.

"Yes, anything! Just keep that bear away from us!"

53

"Have you been dumping pickle juice into the Ice Cream Sea?"

"Who, us? Badness, no. Why would we do such a thing?" The Pickle Necks tried to look innocent.

"So you haven't been dumping pickle juice into the ice cream?"

"No, no. Ask around." Marvin turned to Bert, hovering behind him. "Have we been dumping pickle juice into the ice cream?"

"Not us, Boss. Nossiree. Got the wrong pickles."

"Right." All the other Pickle Necks agreed, nodding their bumpy pickle heads up and down like little green golf balls.

"It wasn't us." Marvin tried to look important, the way a leader should. "We wouldn't dream of dumping our barrels and barrels of pickle juice into such lovely ice cream—would we, boys?"

"Right on, boss."

"Tee-hee," chortled Bert.

"Wrong!" shouted Alula-Belle.

"Huh?"

Alula-Belle would have to be a clever girl to outsmart the Pickle Necks. She took a deep breath. "Are you telling me that the Big Award for dumping pickle juice into the Ice Cream Sea doesn't go to the Pickle Necks?"

"The Big Award?" The Pickle Necks didn't know what to say. They were pickle-tied.

"Well well well well well well well," said Alula-Belle. "No pickle juice, no Big Award." She knew it was impossible to get the truth out of a Pickle Neck. She would have to trick them at their own game.

"The Big Award goes to the ones responsible for dumping pickle juice into the ice cream. If you didn't do it, maybe *we* can claim the award," she teased.

"*You?*"

"Sure, why not? You Pickle Necks say you didn't do it."

"But...but we want the award! We deserve it!" The Pickle Necks grumbled and fussed and poked each other with their elbows.

"Hmm," said Alula-Belle thoughtfully. "If you want the Big Award you must do exactly as I say." (She knew that whatever she said to do, the Pickle Necks would do the exact opposite.) "Do you promise to dump your pickle juice into the Ice Cream Sea?"

"Oh yes. We promise we will dump our pickle juice into the ice cream!" Every one of them crossed their pickle fingers behind their pickle backs.

Alula-Belle stepped forward, squinting her eyes like grown-ups do when they think something costs too much money. "Do you mean to tell me you aren't lying?"

"Us?" yawled Marvin, looking hurt. "Oh, ungracious, no! Never. We never lie."

The others echoed, "No, we never lie."

"We couldn't tell a lie," cackled Bert.

"Lying is bad."

"Our noses would grow if we lied."

"See how small our noses are!"

(Pickle Necks don't have mirrors, so they have no idea how long their noses are. And they are plenty long, as you can see.)

"Where's our Big Award?" Marvin shouted. "Hurry up. Hand it over."

"Just a minute. I want to cover every possible slip-up," said Alula-Belle.

"Oh, there won't be any slip-ups—none at all!" clacked the Pickle Necks.

Alula-Belle had another question. "What

happens to your pickle juice when you don't have any ice cream to dump it into?"

Suddenly, the Pickle Necks looked sad. Bert bounced forward. "You see, we keep our pickle juice in pickle barrels to make pickle pie and pickle cupcakes and pickle peppers. But there are no more pickle trees, so we have no pickle wood to make pickle barrels to store the pickle juice. And without pickle barrels for pickle juice, we can't pickle!"

Which happened to be true. The pickle trees *were* all gone. And without their pickle trees, the Pickle Necks had no pickle wood to build pickle houses, or make pickle paper. There was no pickle wood for pickle chairs, pickle tables, pickle rafts, or pickle slingshots. Without pickle trees, the Pickle Necks were definitely in a pickle.

But to Alula-Belle's way of thinking, no problem was too hard to solve. "Be brave and do hard things, my mother always told me," she whispered confidently to Jo-Jo and Pearl. "Now is our chance."

The Pickle Necks were getting restless.

"What if I told you that I can grow pickle trees?" offered Alula-Belle. "I will plant a Pickle Woods for you."

A gasp went up from the Pickle Necks. "Pickle trees!"

"My pockets are filled with pickle tree seeds. I would be happy to plant them for you. But first you must absolutely promise that you will never stop dumping your pickle juice into the Ice Cream Sea." (Alula-Belle was being very clever.)

"You want us to dump pickle juice into the ice cream? Sure! It's a promise," the Pickle Necks lied, bobbing their bumpy heads up and down.

"Absolutely."

"Not to worry."

"We're Pickle Necks of our word."

Alula-Belle smiled. Her trick was successful. "You will find your Pickle Woods at the edge of Umbrella Forest, where there is a very nice clearing, just perfect for pickle trees to grow. It will be easy for you to find the spot. All you have to do is turn around three times and follow your noses. And before you know it, you'll be there."

The Pickle Necks cheered.

"Tee-hee. We win again!" The Pickle Necks sniggered and slapped one another on their green backs. "We won't add one teensy-weensy drop of pickle juice to their Ice Cream Sea. Then they'll really be angry!"

With that, the Pickle Necks prepared to leave Ice Cream Beach and never come back.

"That monstrous bear won't ever find us far away in our new Pickle Woods! We will keep all our pickle juice in pickle vats! Har. Har."

Quite pleased with themselves, they agreed gleefully that it certainly had been a bad day.

Jo-Jo Peach Jam spoke into Alula-Belle's ear. "It's getting late. We better get going quick." He sounded urgent. Alula-Belle waved goodbye. Jo-Jo held on to his hat. Vera Beara yawned a relieved yawn. Pearl Pox tossed another ice-cream ball at Bert Pickle Neck.

And with that, Alula-Belle, Jo-Jo Peach Jam, Pearl Pox, and Vera Beara soared away into the blue sky.

CHAPTER 8

MORE DANGER AHEAD

But they had left too late. The storm was gathering ahead.

"Vera Beara," asked Jo-Jo Peach Jam, "will you be coming back to Kneebend-on-Limber with us?"

"Yes, come live with us in my beautiful tree house which I built myself," invited Alula-Belle.

"Well, I just don't know," said Vera Beara. "It all depends on what time of year this is...does anybody know when school starts?"

"That's easy," sighed Pearl Pox impatiently. "Everyone knows school starts in September."

"Summer school doesn't start in September," said Vera Beara. "And not year-round school, either. And what about home school? Oh, I'm so confused!"

Pearl Pox hoisted herself into a sit-up-straight position. "School starts when it starts, you silly bear. And for your information, it is now summer. Summer summer summer. You can tell by the weather. When the weather is hot, it must be summer—that is, unless you live in Australia, which you do not."

Vera Beara scratched her head. "But do you have the time? I mean, just as I get used to the idea of it being one o'clock, it's suddenly one minute past. And that means one o'clock is gone. Where did it go?"

Alula-Belle, who had been listening, gave Vera Beara an encouraging nudge. "Come back to Kneebend-on-Limber with us, and I will let you have my clock. You can keep it with you always. That way when it is one o'clock today, you know it will be one o'clock again tomorrow. And it will also be two o'clock and three o'clock. You will have all the time in the world."

"That's right," Jo-Jo said. "You will have time in your hands, so to speak." Jo-Jo and Alula-Belle smiled, and so did Vera Beara. She already felt at home with her new friends.

"I would like very much to come to Kneebend-on-Limber with you," she said. "With or without December."

"Terrific!" said Jo-Jo.

"Hi-dee-ho!" said Alula-Belle.

"Humph," said Pearl Pox.

They flew smoothly through the growing dark clouds and bad weather.

"The sun is getting ready to go to bed," said Jo-Jo Peach Jam, suddenly worried.

Alula-Belle called out to the sun in her friendliest voice, "Hello, Sun! How beautiful you are looking today!"

"You mean *tonight*, Alula-Belle dear. I was just getting ready to go to bed."

"Oh, but, Sun, won't you stay up a little while longer?" Alula-Belle pleaded sweetly. "Please? Just so I can have time enough to fly over the clearing at the edge of Umbrella Forest and drop

"Do hurry. I'm an early riser, you know."

down some pickle tree seeds?"

The sun rubbed her large, golden eyes. "Are you planting pickle trees, Alula-Belle?"

"Yes, for the Pickle Necks, so they will stop pouring pickle juice into the Ice Cream Sea. Will you help the trees to grow?"

"Whatever you plant, I will always help to grow," answered the sun.

"Thank you, Sun."

"But do hurry. I was just getting ready to take my bath so I could crawl under the covers for a good night's sleep. I'm an early riser, you know."

So Alula-Belle flew past the Umbrella Forest to the clearing and planted the pickle tree seeds just as she had promised. When she was finished, the sun winked her eye and slipped under the covers of the crimson horizon.

"Good night," she called before dozing off.

"Oh dear," said Alula-Belle. "I forgot to ask the sun if she would please stay up until we got past the Great Winds and through the storm. Hang on, everyone, we are heading for a bumpy ride."

Pearl Pox gave Vera Beara a shove. "You're hogging up all the room," she snapped. "Alula-Belle, something is sticking me in the ribs. And I want more ice cream! Everyone else got more than me. I'm cold! I'm hot! I'm hungry! I'm full! I'm tired! I'm not tired! Besides, I never heard of anybody who could talk to the sun. Flying is stupid."

It had gotten quite dark. Cousin Fred's warning was coming true. The storm was upon them. The wind was becoming stronger. It was difficult for Alula-Belle to fly against so strong a wind. She began to swerve and sway. "Hang on!" she shouted.

Now they were wobbling and tossing about the sky.

"I've had enough of your pranks, Alula-Belle!" yelled Pearl Pox, hanging on to Vera Beara for dear life. "Riffraff pickles are one thing, a stupid lunk of a bear is another, but flapping and

flopping around in the sky at night is absolutely unacceptable! Take me home!"

Jo-Jo ducked into his shell house. He went to his computer and keyed in to air-traffic control. He pulled on his headset.

"Push to the left. Turn a bit to your right—careful on the upswing," he called out.

Alula-Belle did exactly as Jo-Jo said. But even so, the winds were getting more and more powerful, and Alula-Belle felt herself growing weak. Struggling to keep aloft, her tired arms fell slowly to her sides. The little group plunged downward, until they were tumbling out of control. Down, down, down into the blackness below.

All seemed to be lost.

This would have been the end of the story if it had not been for an astonishing discovery on board. It just goes to show you that sometimes when you think a thing is one way, it turns out to be another. At the moment you think something is totally dreadful, a spark of good shows up. Just when you think all is hopeless, a promising beam of light appears—and help is on its way.

STRANGER ON BOARD

B|ut help doesn't always come in a way you'd expect.

"I feel upside-down sick!" shouted a strange voice.

Up popped the crinkly green head of Bert Pickle Neck. He had sneaked on board just to make sure Alula-Belle kept her promise about

"I feel upside-down sick!" shouted a strange voice.

the pickle trees, but forgot to get off at the proper time. Now he sprang from beneath Pearl's lunch basket with an angry jolt, and when he did, everyone tipped right-side-up again. He jerked and tossed and jumped up and down as though he were sitting on a nest of bees. And every time he jumped, Alula-Belle's arms bounced back up into the air.

This went on for quite a while, until angry old Bert became so furious he fell right off. But instead of falling down like you would have thought, he fell sideways and landed—*kerplop*—right on top of the place he was falling from. With Bert Pickle Neck stretched sideways across the little flying group, it was like having another wing-a-ling. Jo-Jo and Pearl grabbed one end of him, and Vera Beara grabbed the other.

Alula-Belle knew her prayers were answered. She flew and the others steered. "We're getting more lift! We're saved!" cheered Vera Beara.

Jo-Jo called out air-traffic commands. "Open the landing flaps! We're banking and climbing!"

"How much farther?" croaked Pearl Pox.

"We may be flying all night," answered Alula-Belle.

Pearl humphed and phumphed. "I just *knew*

It was like having another wing-a-ling.

"Why, Alula-Belle," said the moon, "what are you doing out on a night like this?"

I'd miss my supper."

The hours went by, and the struggle through the storm continued. At last Alula-Belle saw the moon high above and far away. It looked like a peach with a bite taken out of it. She called out, "Moon! Oh, Moon!"

The moon leaned forward to peer down at the tiny figure and her passengers flying through the stormy sky. "Why, Alula-Belle," said the moon. "What are you doing out on a night like this?"

"Oh, having a pleasant enough time I suppose—considering. Thank you very much," said Alula-Belle, trying hard to sound cheerful. "I was wondering, though, could you loan me a star or two?"

"Bad timing, dear girl," said the moon. "Every star in the galaxy is burnt out tonight. Haven't you noticed? Not a star in the sky."

"Yes, I noticed."

The moon was a temperamental sort. Sometimes he could be downright ornery and stubborn. Alula-Belle could see that tonight he was feeling a little moody, a little pesky. Maybe because he could hardly be seen in the storm. (The moon is vain, you know, and likes to be admired and appreciated. He prefers to light up the night world with a silvery glow and not be stuck away behind some big black cloud until morning.)

"Say, who have you got on board there? Do I see a Pickle Neck?"

"Pickle Necks are horrible and awful!" shouted Pearl Pox. "They dump pickle juice into ice cream!"

Alula Belle had an idea. She said to the moon, "Oh, but this one is a special Pickle Neck. He is unlike any other Pickle Neck in the world. If you were just a little closer, you could take a look."

Old Bert Pickle Neck was stuck flying sideways. He was so shaken up, he couldn't say a word—which was just as well.

The moon, who is a very curious type and loves to check things out, sighed a curious sigh. Then he rolled onto the curve of his back and zoomed down—right next to Alula-Belle in her perilous flight.

"Where is he?" asked the moon.

"Come closer," Alula-Belle said, and when the moon drew closer, she grabbed hold of his pointed end. "Now, hurry ahead while I tell you a secret." (If there's anything the moon enjoys, it's a juicy secret.)

"Oh goodie, a secret! Tell. Do tell," he begged, merrily pulling Alula-Belle and her cargo along.

Tonight the moon was feeling a little moody, a little pesky.

Without knowing it, the moon was rapidly towing them out of the storm.

"A little faster," Alula-Belle urged. The moon pulled faster, and Alula-Belle rested her arms. "Moon, you said you were short of stars tonight, didn't you?"

The moon nodded his pointed head. "That's right."

"Well, don't look now, but this Pickle Neck on board happens to be quite old. As far as I can see, he's exhausted from roaming around the world getting into trouble."

The moon sneaked a peek at Bert Pickle Neck, who had gotten something in his eye and was miserably rubbing his lumpy green forehead.

Alula-Belle continued. "So what do you say you stick him up in the sky? You could give him a job as a part-time traffic light. You know, for nights like this."

"Let's have a better look at him," said the moon, swooping around to have another peek at mean old Bert Pickle Neck, who was now busy thinking up sideways lies.

"I'll take him," said the moon. "I have just the place for his sort."

"Good riddance!" shouted Pearl Pox.

"I'll take him. I have just the place for his sort."

With that, the moon gathered up Bert Pickle Neck and carried him off into the black night.

C H A P T E R

So Long Bert!

They were now out of danger, for the moon had pulled them clear through to the end of the storm. Everyone watched as the moon became farther and farther away. Then, in the far-away distance, the tiniest dull green spot appeared. It was in the blackest corner of the sky, far away from the moon and the other stars.

"There's nobody to lie to up there," said Jo-Jo. "Just the night air."

(So when you look up at the night sky and see a little green flicker, dull as can be—in fact, you'll think you didn't even see it, but there it will be, blinkering away in the night—it's not a star, or a comet, or another planet. No, it's just old Bert Pickle Neck moping around in the sky and wishing he had somebody to lie to. Not many space travelers pay much attention to a pickle hanging around the galaxy trying to direct traffic.)

Which only goes to prove that dishonest, mean pickles almost always come to a sorry end.

Alula-Belle heard later that the other Pickle Necks had gone into the bubble gum business and were pickling bubble gum all over Australia.

Oh. I almost forgot to tell you this part. The rest of the trip back to Kneebend-on-Limber went as smooth as candy. Alula-Belle and her friends sailed through the air with the greatest of ease. In the middle of their flight, when they had reached cruising altitude, they met with the gentlest of rain. Everyone got wet and enjoyed the rain as it washed everything clean.

Jo-Jo Peach Jam gave Pearl Pox a tiny turtle grin. "See? I told you Alula-Belle could fly as far

as the rain."

Pearl had to admit that Alula-Belle could do practically anything. "Anything, that is, except get me home in time for supper."

And she was plenty mad.

About the Author

Marie Jordan Chapian is well loved around the world as an inspirational author and speaker. Her books have sold over two million copies. The Alula-Belle series was inspired by Marie's performances, stories and puppet shows for children, which she presents both live and for television and radio. As an artist, Marie's paintings have been shown in galleries in the United States and Europe and her whimsical illustrations have appeared in major magazines. She has won several awards as an author, playwright, poet, and designer, including the Cornerstone Book of the Year Award, the Gold Medallion, and the Chicago News Book of the Year Award. She currently lives in southern California.